Parrot in
the Bat's Cave

Written by Jill Eggleton
Illustrated by Richard Hoit

Parrot went into a cave.
A bat was in the cave.

"Are you a bat?"
said the bat.

"No, I'm a parrot,"
said Parrot.

3

The bat went
up to Parrot.

"You are in this cave,"
he said.
"You are a bat."

The bat got up
on the wall.

"Come on,"
said the bat.
"Come up here
like me.
You are a bat."

Parrot went up
on the wall
like the bat.

"Eeek!" she said.
"Eeek! Eeek!"

9

The bat looked
at Parrot.
"Shhhh," he said.
"Go to sleep."

"Eeek! Eeek! Eeek!"
said Parrot.
"I can't go to sleep!"

The bat was mad!

"**Shoo!**" he said.
"You are not a bat.
Go away!"

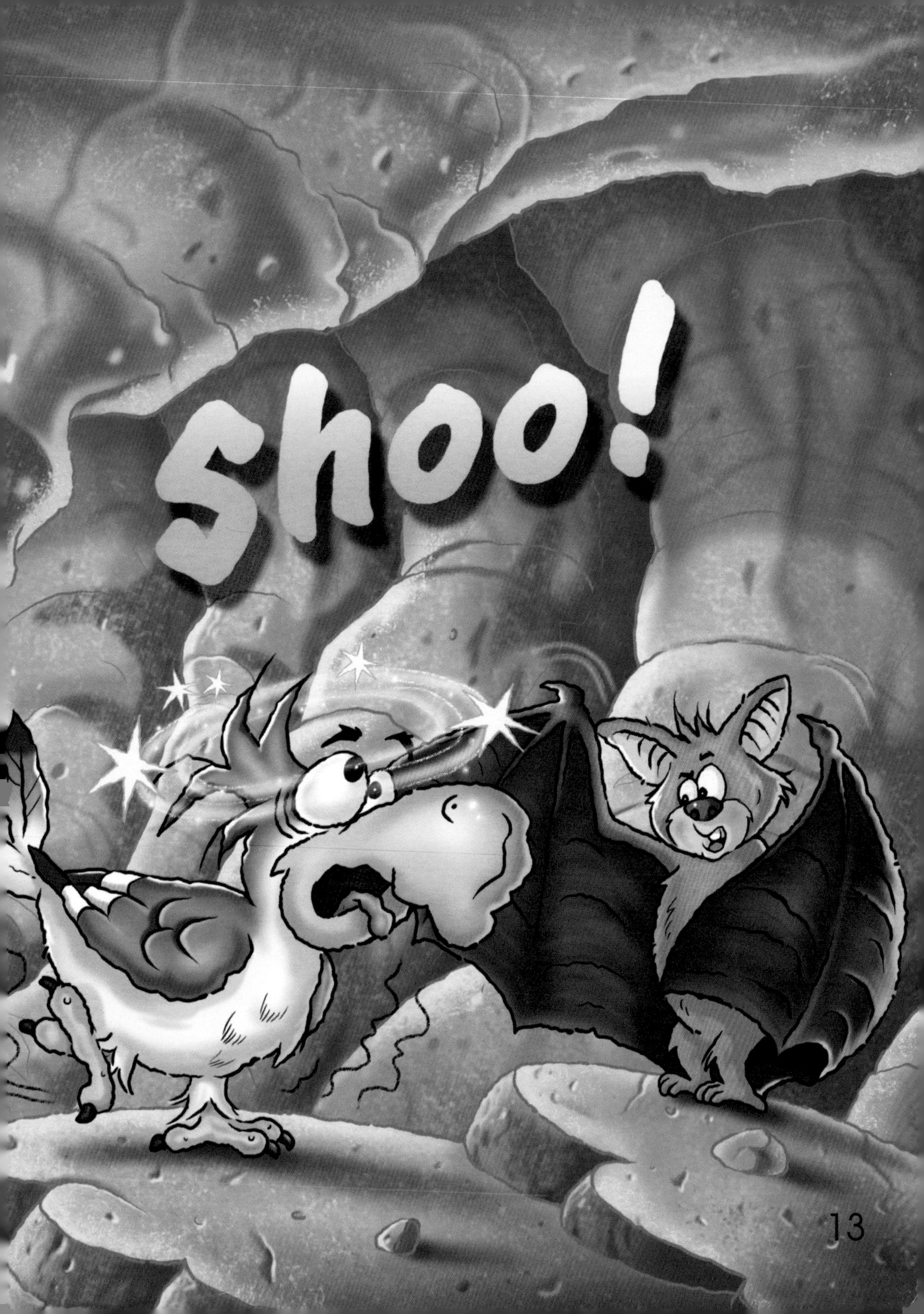
Shoo!

Parrot went away.
"Silly bat," she said.
"Look at me!
I am **not** a bat.
I am a parrot!"

Rules

Rules in this cave

- Stay upside down.
- No going eeeek.
- No parrots.

Guide Notes

Title: Parrot in the Bat's Cave
Stage: Early (2) - Yellow

Genre: Fiction
Approach: Guided Reading
Processes: Thinking Critically, Exploring Language, Processing Information
Written and Visual Focus: Rules
Word Count: 130

THINKING CRITICALLY
(sample questions)
- What do you think this story could be about?
- Focus on the title and discuss.
- Why do you think Parrot went into the bat's cave?
- How do you know Parrot didn't like being up on the wall?
- Why do you think the bat couldn't go to sleep?
- Why do you think Parrot couldn't go to sleep?
- Where do you think Parrot could have gone to sleep?

EXPLORING LANGUAGE

Terminology
Title, cover, illustrations, author, illustrator

Vocabulary
Interest words: cave, silly, parrot, bat, eeek, shoo
High-frequency words: away, was, can't, I'm
Positional words: into, in, up, on

Print Conventions
Capital letter for sentence beginnings and names (**P**arrot), periods, commas, quotation marks, exclamation marks, question mark